It's Mine!

This Book Belongs To:

_____

Visit us on the Web! randomhousekids.com
Kohls.com/Kids
Educators and librarians, for a variety of teaching tools, visit us at
RHTeachersLibrarians.com

This special edition was printed for Kohl's Department Stores, Inc.
(for distribution on behalf of Kohl's Cares, LLC, its wholly owned subsidiary),
by Random House Children's Books, a division of Penguin Random House LLC,
New York.

Kohl's
1415114-00
123387
08/15 – 10/15

ISBN 978-0-375-97504-2
MANUFACTURED IN CHINA
10 9 8 7 6 5 4 3 2 1

It's Mine!

by Leo Lionni

Alfred A. Knopf 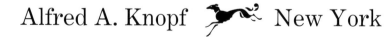 New York

In the middle of Rainbow Pond
there was a small island.
Smooth pebbles lined its beaches,
and it was covered with ferns
and leafy weeds.

On the island lived three quarrelsome frogs named Milton, Rupert, and Lydia. They quarreled and quibbled from dawn to dusk.

"Stay out of the pond!" yelled Milton. "The water is mine."

"Get off the island!" shouted Rupert. "The earth is mine."

"The air is mine!" screamed Lydia as she leaped
to catch a butterfly. And so it went.

One day a large toad appeared before them.

"I live on the other side of the island," he said, "but I can hear you shouting 'It's mine! It's mine! It's mine!' all day long. There is no peace because of your endless bickering. You can't go on like this!" With that the toad slowly turned around and hopped away through the weeds.

No sooner had he left than Milton ran off with a large worm. The others hopped after him. "Worms are for everybody!" they cried.

But Milton croaked defiantly, "Not this one. It's mine!"

Suddenly the sky darkened and a rumble
of distant thunder circled the island.
Rain filled the air, and the water turned to
mud. The island grew smaller and smaller
as it was swallowed up by the rising
flood. The frogs were scared.

Desperately they clung to the few
slippery stones that still rose above the
wild, dark water. But soon these too
began to disappear.

There was only one rock left and there the frogs huddled, trembling from cold and fright. But they felt better now that they were together, sharing the same fears and hopes. Little by little the flood subsided. The rain fell gently and then stopped altogether.

But look! The large rock that had saved them was no rock at all.
    "You saved us!" shouted the frogs when they recognized the toad.

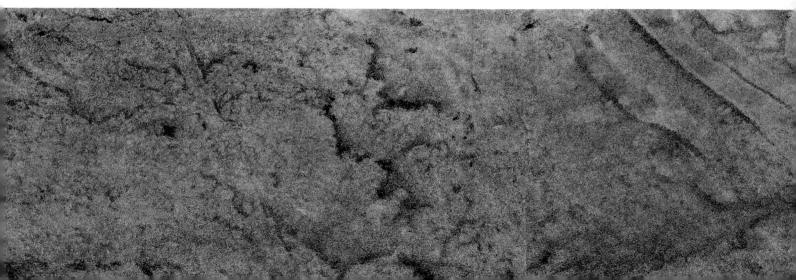

The next morning the water had cleared. Sunrays
chased silver minnows on the sandy bottom of the pond.
Joyfully the frogs jumped in, and side by side
they swam all around the island.

Together they leaped after the swarms of butterflies that filled the air.

And later, when they rested in the weeds, they felt happy in a way they had never been before.

"Isn't it peaceful," said Milton.

"And isn't it beautiful," said Rupert.

"And do you know what else?" said Lydia.

"No, what?" the others asked.

"It's ours!" she said.